FRUITS vs. VEGGIES

BY : The Thompson Family

Illustrated By : Natasha Bolonna

This is a work of fiction.

Names, characters, places and incidents either are the product of the author's imagination or are used fictitiously. Any resemblance to actual persons, living or dead, events or locales is entirely coincidental.

Fruits vs. Veggies

Published by ICJ publishing in the United States
thompsonfamilycreation.com

Do you believe that food can talk?

Well, start believing! I'm a talking Tomato.

First, let me introduce myself. My name is Tiny. It is spelled T-I-N-Y. My full name is Tiny the Tomato, but don't let the name fool you; I am a proud, ripe, red tomato who loves to write epic stories.

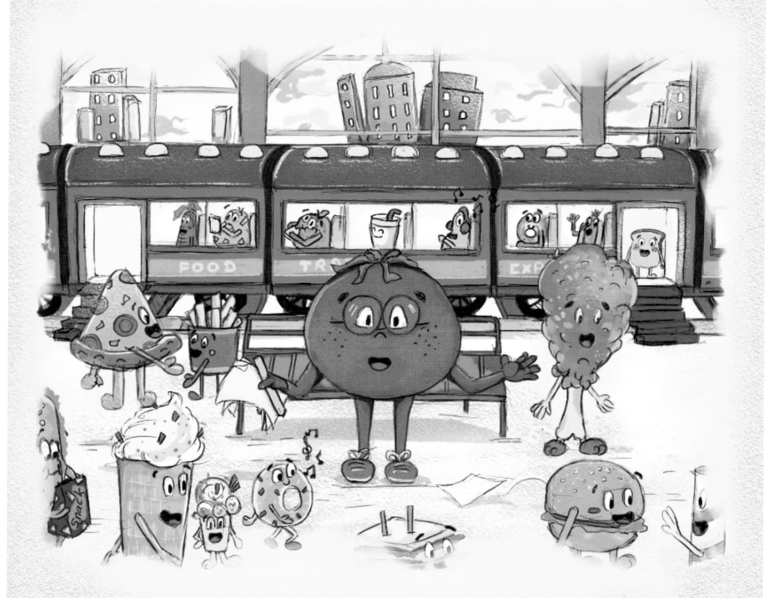

Let me tell you a little secret. I've written the most epic story ever, but... at first, I didn't know what to write about or where to start.

So, I climbed aboard the Food Train Express and visited the most famous cities to get inspired. I'm going to tell you about my journey!

Wait! I need to do the most important thing before I begin telling my story.

Let's pray, "Dear God, thank you for your love and protection for all creation. Please help guide me in my purpose to follow your way. I love you, in Jesus' name, amen."

I had my pen and notepad ready to start my mission for the G.S.O.F.H., aka the "Greatest Story of Food History."

I just had to see if there was a story to be told out there.

As the Food Train Express started to leave the station, the ticket holder said, "Tickets! Tickets! All aboard! Hop on the Food Train Express and explore.

First stop... Meat Metropolis."

My first stop was Meat Metropolis. I'd heard about this city. My friend Bacon and his little brother Ham live there. One time, I met the band called Terry T-Bone and the Steaks. They are famous country singers. They sing the song, "Love Meat Tender." Meats come from all around the city to see the band, but the concerts are all grilled out. I have to say, Meat Metropolis was a bustling and fast-paced city. I couldn't keep up with all the meaty meats. All I managed to write down was that they love the heat and staying fit.

There were great stories to write about Meat Metropolis, but I didn't find the Greatest Story of Food History.

As I boarded the train and sat in my seat, the ticket holder yelled, "Tickets, Tickets! All aboard! Hop on the Food Train Express and explore. Second stop... Sweet Cream City."

The next stop was Sweet Cream City. It was in a place called Freezer County.

Weird, right? Ice cream, popsicles, and all types of frozen treats live here. This place was pretty "cool." It was always snowing, and it even had a giant ice castle. Lots of the goodies were sweet, but some were sour. There were lots of beautiful ideas to write about, but brrrr!! I couldn't stay there too long. I loved the sweet treats of Sweet Cream City, but... it was just too cold to write the G.S.O.F.H. there. I would have been a frozen tomato ball.

I heard the Food Train Express whistle as it left the station. Oh no! The train was going to leave without me, and I was too slow! "Wait! Wait! Please don't leave!"

I shouted after the train. There was still so much more I needed to see. Then I felt a hand reaching out for me. He pulled me up into the train and introduced himself by saying his name.

He said loud and proud, "Howdy, buddy, I am Chippity Chip Cookie, but everyone calls me Chip. What's got you in such a hurry?"

I replied, "I'm searching for a great and epic story to write about that will change food history."

The ticket holder then shouted, "Tickets! Tickets! All aboard! Hop on the Food Train Express and explore. Third stop… Dessert City."

Chip yelled, "Chocolatey chipping cookies! Well, partner, look no further. You need to write your story in this here town."

The third stop was Dessert City. As I stepped off the train, I was greeted with the sweet smells of chocolate with hints of vanilla and cinnamon. I started to make my way into the city, and I was interrupted by bright flashing lights and reporters screaming to take pictures of the premier models Cherry Cheesecake and Milo Macaroon. Hmmm... I thought this place had the story I'd been searching for. I tried and tried to shuffle my way to the front of the crowd. I went left and couldn't find my way. I ran to the right, and I fell on my face. I was too small to see anything.

There were many great stories about Dessert City, but I still needed a different and unique story. It was time to go back to the train. I was determined to find the perfect story.

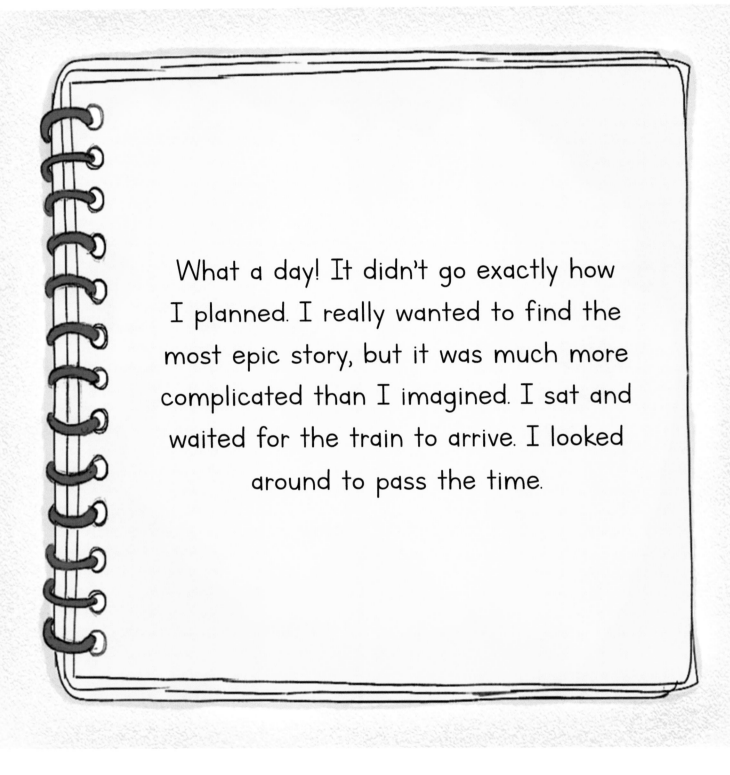

What a day! It didn't go exactly how I planned. I really wanted to find the most epic story, but it was much more complicated than I imagined. I sat and waited for the train to arrive. I looked around to pass the time.

Then, suddenly, I saw it. I saw what looked like the biggest event of the year. It was a massive tug of war game. It was fruits vs. veggies. It was going to be amazing! I just knew I had to get there!

I decided to board the Food Train Express once more. I knew I had finally found the story that I had been looking for.

I took my seat and heard the ticket holder repeat, "Tickets! Tickets! All aboard! Hop on the Food Train Express and explore! Last stop... Produce County. The ticket holder came toward me and introduced himself. He said, "Why, hello! My name is Al Avocado. I've seen you a lot today. You've been one busy tomato. Have you decided where you would like to stay?"

I replied, "A long day I've had indeed, but there is still one more place I need to see. I've searched these cities to find the greatest story of all time!"

"Well, you know, there's this big event at our next stop. It's a tug of war game between the fruits and the veggies. I'm sure a story like this is a rare opportunity. But, I must say, there is history to this story that has gone on for centuries. The big feud between Veggie Land and Fruit City has become the biggest mystery. No one knows how it began. After all of these generations, I wonder when this feud will end."

As the train pulled into the stop, I took a deep breath and thought, Okay, Tiny. This is the last stop. I may be a little nervous to start my story, but I need to remember this promise of God: "I can do all things through Christ who gives me strength," Philippians 4:13. With my pen and paper in hand, I confidently walked into Produce County, home to Fruit City and Veggie Land.

Let me tell you, these cities were so beautiful they made my cheeks turn pink. I couldn't believe my eyes. I couldn't believe what I saw. Fruit City was the definition of fun and adventure. There was a Zippy Seed Zip Line, Sunrays Café, and Fructose T.V., which always had the latest episodes of the sweetest and silliest cartoons. Then there was Veggie Land, which had many beautiful parks and botanical gardens. These peaceful gardens overlooked a gorgeous waterfall that flowed into the valley. The Leafy Green Library had all the most exciting books you could ever read.

In between these two great cities, there was an untouched valley. It had luscious green grass and a peaceful lake that rested in the middle. As I walked into the valley, I saw hundreds of fruits and vegetables prepping for the tug of war game. Then a tomato just like me approached and said, "Tomato-tomahto! Why, hello, my friend! Let me introduce myself. My name is Rufus. I'm the mayor of both of these cities in Produce County. Did you come for the big game?"

I said, "Yes! I love Produce County, Mayor Rufus. My name is Tiny. I'm a writer and I'm searching for the next big story. This game interests me. Can you tell me how it came to be?"

Mayor Rufus replied, "Well, Tiny, this land we're standing on is called Garden Valley. The tug of war game is a competition to see which city gets to have this beautiful land. After all these years of disagreement about how to use Garden Valley, the matter will be finally settled by the tug of war game today. If the fruits win, they want to make a fruitastic amusement park. If the veggies win, they want to build a top-level prep school. You should stick around and see who the winner will be. Oh shucks! I have to go. Nice talking with you, Tiny. Enjoy the show."

Then the big game finally began. "Fruits, Fruits, Fruits!"

"Veggies, Veggies, Veggies!"

These were the sounds that roared from the citizens of Food World as the players gathered at both ends of the rope. I then heard a voice say, "Ready... Set... Go...!" First, the fruits snatched the rope, and the veggies pulled. Then the veggies tugged, and the fruits jerked it back. Both sides pulled the rope with all their might, and then... SNAP! THE ROPE BROKE! Oh my tomatoes! I'm so glad I wrote all this down on my notepad, I never would have remembered it all!

I was still writing while there was confusion in the crowd. Some said the fruits won while others said that the veggies won. Mayor Rufus walked on stage with a piece of paper with the results to announce who won the game. He opened the envelope and said, "We have a two-way tie!"

Mayor Rufus continued, "I know you may have expected different results today, but maybe we should look at this disagreement in a new way. If we all really want the best for this beautiful land, why can't we share and be friends? Hebrews 13:16 says, 'Do not neglect to do good and share what you have, for such sacrifices are pleasing to God.' So, don't you see it's not right for us to be mean? Let's change past mistakes and make them present victories."

I was in awe as I made my way back to the train. Everyone was overcome with joy and love as they agreed with Mayor Rufus' wise words. The fruits and veggies wanted a change, so they decided to sign a peace treaty. Produce County would no longer be divided. It would be unified with God's guidance. Who knew that I could learn so much through my journey that day. I went in search of the Greatest Story of Food History, but I got so much more than a simple story.

When I first got to Produce County, I expected that either the fruits or the veggies were going to win the tug of war, but the game turned out to be more than just an event. The lesson I learned gave me so much more understanding. I knew then that my story needed to teach and not just tell the word of God. I really did find the G.S.O.F.H, but I didn't write about some tug of war game. I wrote about love and kindness and how they're an expression of God's glory.

FRUCTOSE NEWSPAPER

Food World's
Best-Selling
Author

Tiny
Tomato

About the author

Who says a family can't write children books together? ! Hello, we are The Thompson Family! Micheal Sr., Earnice, Ermya, Micheal Jr., Emeri and McKenzie. We are a family of six, each with our own personality, that love to write Christ-centered stories for the whole family to enjoy. You see it all started with deciding to pray together as a family which developed into what we now call family night. We used our family nights to connect with each other and the beauty of God's word. This produced a load of wonderful and creative writings inspired by God that are purposeful and fun to read.